MOMENTS IN A FLASH

TALES OF LIFE AND WONDER

DR. SRABANI BASU

Made with ♥ on the Notion Press Platform
www.notionpress.com

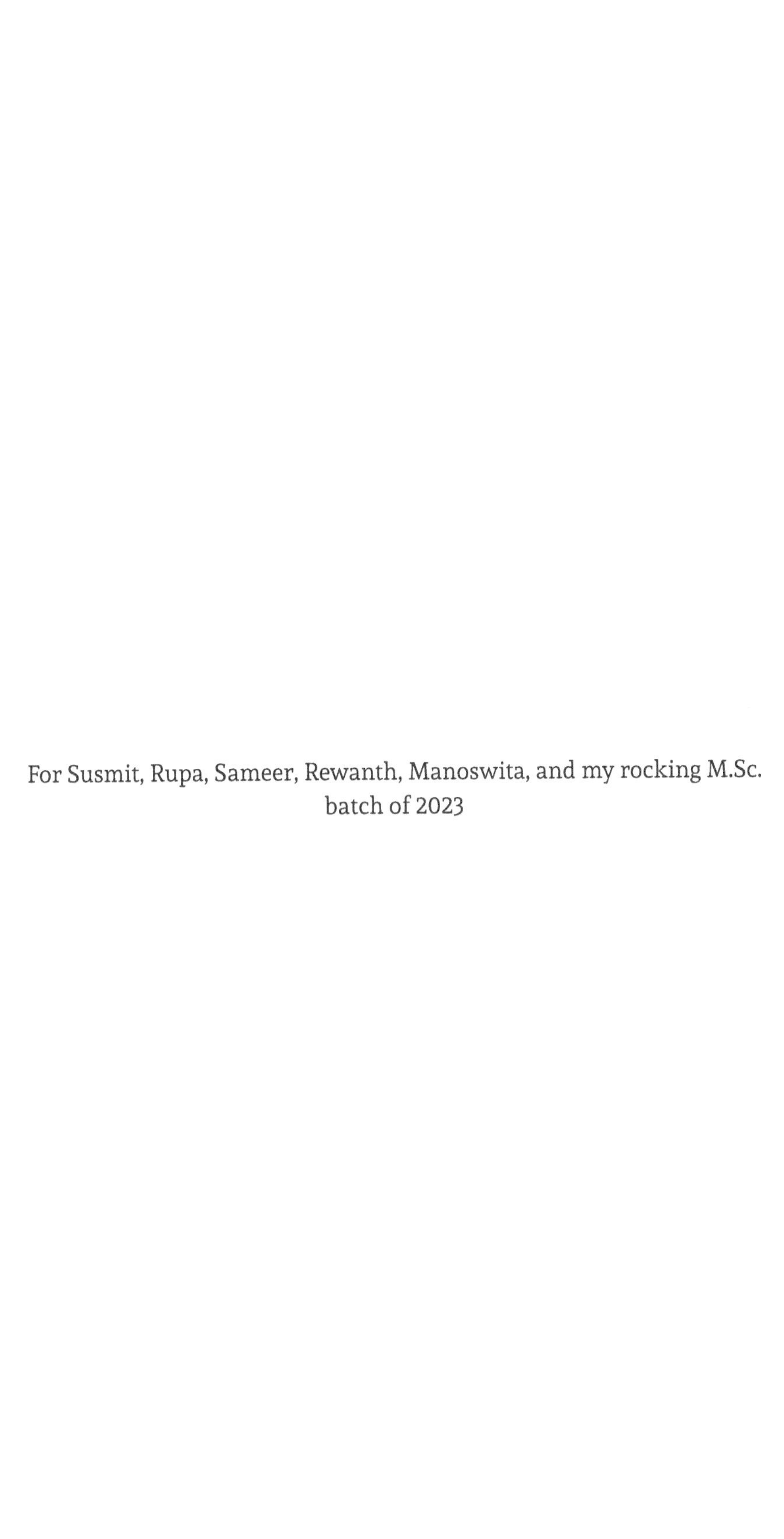

For Susmit, Rupa, Sameer, Rewanth, Manoswita, and my rocking M.Sc. batch of 2023

Contents

PREFACE

The art of storytelling has always fascinated me since my childhood. Growing up, I was captivated by the magic of words, the way they could transport me to different worlds, introduce me to a myriad of characters, and make me experience emotions I had never felt before. Among all the literary genres, flash fiction holds a special place in my heart. It is a genre that demands brevity yet offers boundless opportunities for depth and complexity. It is within this compact form that I have found the perfect vessel to communicate my thoughts and views on various aspects of life.

In this collection of twenty-one flash fictions, I have sought to explore the breadth of human experience through stories that range from the charming and whimsical to the profound and introspective. The beauty of flash fiction lies in its ability to distil a moment, a feeling, or an idea into a few potent words. It is like capturing lightning in a bottle, where every word, every sentence, is charged with meaning and emotion. This form allows me to convey complex ideas and emotions succinctly, making each story a concentrated burst of narrative and thematic richness.

Fairy tales have always held a special charm for me. Their timeless appeal and universal themes resonate deeply with readers of all ages. In this collection, I have included stories that draw on the enchanting world of fairy tales, weaving modern sensibilities with traditional motifs. Fairy tales have a unique ability to speak to the child in all of us, reminding us of the wonder and magic that exists in the world. They also serve as powerful metaphors for the struggles and triumphs we face in our own lives. Through these tales, I hope to evoke a sense of nostalgia and wonder while also offering new perspectives on familiar themes.

Mythology has also been a significant influence on my writing. The rich tapestry of myths from different cultures provides a fertile ground for exploring human nature, morality, and the mysteries of existence. In this collection, I have incorporated elements of mythology to create stories that resonate on a deeper level. Mythological references serve as a bridge between the ancient and the contemporary, allowing me to draw parallels between timeless truths and modern dilemmas. Through these stories, I aim to highlight the enduring relevance of myths and their ability to illuminate the human condition.

Symbolism and imagery are integral to my storytelling. They allow me to convey complex ideas and emotions in a subtle and evocative manner. In these flash fictions, I have used symbolism to add layers of meaning and enrich the reader's experience. Whether it is the use of a broken clock to signify the passage of time and the weight of memories or a withered lilac to represent lost love, these symbols enhance the narrative and invite readers to delve deeper into the stories. Imagery, on the other hand, brings the stories to life, painting vivid pictures that linger in the reader's mind long after the story is finished.

Perspectives play a crucial role in shaping our understanding of the world. In this collection, I have experimented with different narrative perspectives to offer fresh insights and challenge conventional viewpoints. By stepping into the shoes of diverse characters, I hope to foster empathy and broaden the reader's horizons. Whether it is a single mother braving the responsibilities all alone or a buffalo reminiscing about a bygone era, these varied perspectives provide a window into different lives and experiences, enriching the overall tapestry of the collection.

The process of writing these flash fictions has been a journey of discovery and introspection. Each story has allowed me to explore different facets of the human experience, from love and loss to hope and despair. The brevity of the form has compelled me to distil these themes to their essence, resulting in stories that are both concise and impactful. It is my hope that readers will find these stories as engaging and thought-provoking as I have found them to write.

Flash fiction, by its very nature, demands active participation from the reader. It invites them to fill in the gaps, to read between the lines, and to bring their own interpretations to the story. This collaborative aspect of the genre is something I deeply cherish. It creates a dynamic relationship between the writer and the reader, where the story continues to evolve with each new reading. I encourage readers to immerse themselves in these stories, to reflect on their meanings, and to find their own connections and resonances.

This collection is a testament to my love for flash fiction and my belief in its power to capture the essence of life. Through these stories, I have sought to explore the beauty and complexity of the human experience, using the tools of mythology, symbolism, and varied perspectives. It is my hope that these tales will not only entertain but also provoke thought and reflection, leaving a lasting impression on the reader's mind.

As you journey through these stories, I invite you to embrace the magic of fairy tales, the wisdom of myths, and the richness of human experience. Allow yourself to be transported to different worlds, to see through the eyes of diverse characters, and to uncover the deeper meanings woven into the fabric of these narratives. Whether you read them all at once or savour them one by one, I hope you find in these stories a source of inspiration, wonder, and contemplation.

Precisely, this collection of flash fictions is a heartfelt endeavour, born out of a deep appreciation for the genre and a desire to share my thoughts and views on life through the art of storytelling. It is my hope that these stories will resonate with readers, offering them moments of reflection, joy, and insight. Thank you for embarking on this journey with me, and may these tales leave an indelible mark on your heart and mind.

Dr. Srabani Basu

FOREWORD

I am essentially a storyteller, not a teacher of stories, but an avid reader. While reading the flash fictions by my friend Dr. Srabani Basu, I felt the heart of the writer, the heart of the woman, the heart of the earth, the heart of the grass, the heart of the child, the heart of pain, and the heart of fire—all sometimes seem to be one! Heart is a metaphor for blood and flesh, tinged with some darkness and some mystery; if I ascend a little, I meet the brain. Absolutely non-metallic in nature. All of them comprise something which, when explained, is lost, and when understood, cannot be found. If you die again, everything is ruined, even if it goes to the crematorium. So where are the dreams?

I know these are the words of detachment, the dispassion that arises when I see a crematorium. I feel the same when I see a book of stories and poems. How much is in the book? It is difficult to say what does not exist. After the publication of my first book, it seemed like a surprise; I never thought it would happen! Is it true? Placed it on the cheek, placed it on the mouth, smelt it, saw it from a distance, brought it closer. Touched my name gently. Is it true? Or is this a dream?

One day we forget all these dream-reality dizzying tensions. I do not know the name of this love. Nothing matches life. But still, occasionally I remember; in the heart of the subconscious remains something priceless, which will remain even after we merge the five element, even if it is devalued. Literature is such a resource, perhaps.

However, some voracious readers can even destroy some books with a blink of an eye. They are esteemed. I can't do that. For me, one book is like one person, one personality, one direction, one philosophy. For me, one book is one galaxy. Blood, flesh, fire, tears, sweat, woven in the calligraphy of dreams, a carpet to fly to the planet. It is God's face leaning on the triangular joint in thirst to drink poison — his longing — poetry! It cannot be denied: when it comes to literature, the mind's fervour is ignited! Plato seemed to understand this well. He described poets as lacking theory and logic, yet literature is far from devoid of truth. He beautifully captured this essence, stating, 'These souls flying like bees from flower to flower and wandering over the gardens and meadows and the honey-flowing fountains of the Muses return to us laden with the sweetness of melody.'

Plato articulated this at least four centuries before the birth of Christ. His words have not been erased from the world; they are eternal. However, in the minds of today's literary artists, many more concepts, truths, facts, and theories are gradually being revealed. Sociology, physiology, materialism and its contradictions, and the death of the mind continually unsettle and accelerate the creativity of this period.

Srabani writes her stories exploring complex aspects of modern life. In the first story, a young lady meets a friend in a coffee shop who had scores of affairs, endless women, and a couple of real heartbreaks. He liked women only to the extent to which they did not make him feel responsible or smothered. Thus, he liked her. She was just a friend, and thankfully, neither of them had ever had any romantic illusions about each other to tarnish that friendship. The lady loves a person who, according to her, doesn't love her. But she feels very happy with him as he cares for her much more than all those people who claimed to have loved her. She had not come here looking for sympathy or help. She had just come to share a cup of coffee with an old friend in the city. She left without tarrying any further. She paid for the coffee and made a dash. Getting out of the coffee shop, she landed on a sidewalk teeming with people. She would be here somewhere, he thought, making her way towards her car. Then he saw her... a small head bobbing up and down. Her confident yet speedy gait was a dead giveaway. Her form was unmistakable to him. Even from a distance, he could not have missed her. She would be crying once she was inside the car. This was something he knew. Wasn't that what friends did... they knew you, even if you thought they did not? He smiled to himself as a prayer issued from his lips. He hoped for it to be answered. He turned around and started walking the other way in search of his car. He had a home to go back to.

As I read these stories, I felt that the frenzy of sound and visuals sometimes overwhelmed each other, or that the visuals themselves became suicidal in their exhilaration. However, it is not about the absence of style in the composition; it is about moderation, expression, and the theory of smooth art.

Among the 21 stories in this collection, very few are commercial in nature, while others are emotional. Reading the rest, two trends will be seen. However, despite hundreds of denials, it must be accepted that no matter how commercial the story or literature is, its construction talks about a secret truth felt by the artist who created it. And because of art, there is some automatic discipline. Formal differences. Every art has a rumour, a secret. Literary artists have captured it in different ways. One day the steering of the speech turns to the story, the story turns to the poem, the poem gradually travels towards silence! So, every poet and speaker are basically lonely! In Srabani's stories, that loneliness seems to be a little stronger.

Almost every one of her works has a hint of wistfulness, directly or indirectly, woven into the silken threads of silver and gold. In each story, her boundless repertoire of words and vivid scenes showcases a rich tapestry of imagination and experience. Her unique touch breathes life into every narrative, making each performance unforgettable. As a reader, I am filled with optimism about this storyteller. Her far-reaching imagination and sharp execution have the potential to unlock countless new worlds.

Shyamal Bhattacharya
Kolkata

Acknowledgements

Creating Moments in a Flash: Tales of Life and Wonder has been an incredible journey, one that would not have been possible without the support, guidance, and inspiration of many wonderful individuals.

First and foremost, I would like to express my gratitude to my 7-year-old son, Upamanyu. Your unwavering support and understanding have been my greatest source of strength. Thank you for not seeking my attention while I weaved these stories, and for understanding the late nights when you had to go to bed alone.

A special thanks to my celebrity novelist friend Shyamal Bhattacharya, who inspite of his busy schedule devoted time to review each story, and for writing the foreword. I am truly honoured and can never thank you enough.

To my friend Subhro Sarvin, who have been my sounding board and critic, thank you for your honest feedback and encouragement. Your insights have been invaluable, helping to shape these stories into what they are today. And most importantly for designing the cover page.

My deepest gratitude goes to my mentor, Anil Thomas, whose mastery in storytelling has been a tremendous inspiration for me to continue writing and exploring the depths of this art.

I

The Dandelion

Sunlight filtered through the worn curtains, casting a warm, golden hue across the small, cluttered living room. In the midst of the chaos—an assortment of toys, laundry, and half-read books—stood Ananya, a single mother in her early thirties. Her hands were submerged in soapy water as she washed the breakfast dishes, her mind a whirl of tasks yet to be completed.

"Mommy, look!" came the excited voice of her seven-year-old son, Rishi. Ananya turned to see him standing at the doorway, a proud grin stretching across his sun dappled face. In his small hands, he held a dandelion, its fluffy seeds quivering with the slightest movement.

"That's beautiful, sweetheart," Ananya said, drying her hands on a dish towel. She knelt to his level, brushing a lock of her auburn hair behind her ear. "Where did you find it?"

"By the sidewalk!" Rishi said, his eyes shining with the pure joy of a child. "I picked it for you."

Ananya felt a lump in her throat. It was just a weed, but to Rishi, it was a treasure. "Thank you, Rishi. It's perfect." She kissed his forehead, her heart swelling with a mix of love and melancholy.

Rishi beamed and ran off, the sound of his laughter filling the small apartment. Ananya stood, the dandelion in her hand, and walked to the small table by the window. She placed it in a glass of water, its yellow petals bright against the dimness of the room.

Ananya's thoughts drifted as she stared at the dandelion. She remembered how her life had changed seven years ago when she found out she was pregnant. Rishi's father had left, unable to handle the responsibility. Ananya had been terrified, but the moment she held Rishi in her arms, she knew she would do anything for him.

The years had been a blur of sleepless nights, scraped knees, and whispered bedtime stories. She had juggled multiple jobs, faced endless struggles, and endured loneliness. But through it all, Rishi had been her light, her reason to keep going.

A knock at the door startled her from her reverie. Ananya glanced at the clock—11:00 a.m. She wasn't expecting anyone. Wiping her hands on her jeans, she walked to the door and opened it.

"Hi, Ananya," said Mrs. Basu, her elderly neighbor from across the hall. She held a tray of cookies, the sweet aroma wafting into the apartment. "I thought you and Rishi might like some of these. Just baked them this morning."

Ananya smiled warmly. "Thank you so much, Mrs. Basu. That's very kind of you. Would you like to come in for a bit?"

Mrs. Basu nodded and stepped inside, her eyes crinkling at the corners as she looked around. "You always make this place feel so homey, dear."

"Well, it's home," Ananya replied, leading her to the kitchen. "Can I get you some tea?"

"That would be lovely," Mrs. Basu said, settling into a chair.

Ananya busied herself making tea, grateful for the company. She often felt isolated, her world revolving around Rishi and her work. Mrs. Basu had been a blessing, offering help and companionship whenever she could.

"How's Rishi doing?" Mrs. Basu asked, breaking a cookie in half.

"He's doing well," Ananya said, pouring hot water into two mugs. "Growing up too fast. Sometimes I wish I could slow down time, just a little."

Mrs. Basu chuckled. "They do grow up quickly, don't they? My own children are all grown and have children of their own now. Cherish these moments, Ananya. They pass by in the blink of an eye."

Ananya nodded, bringing the tea to the table. "I try to. It's not always easy, but I try."

They sipped their tea in comfortable silence, the morning sun creeping higher in the sky. Ananya glanced at the dandelion on the table and felt a surge of determination. She would make it through, for Rishi. She would find a way to provide a better life for them both.

"Thank you for the cookies, Mrs. Basu," Ananya said, her voice soft but resolute. "And for being such a good friend."

Mrs. Basu reached across the table and squeezed Ananya's hand. "You're a wonderful mother, Ananya. Don't ever doubt that. And remember, it's okay to ask for help when you need it."

Ananya nodded, tears pricking at the corners of her eyes. "I will. Thank you."

After Mrs. Basu left, Ananya sat by the window, watching Rishi play in the courtyard below. His laughter drifted up to her, a reminder of all the joy and innocence in the world. She took a deep breath, feeling a sense of peace settle over her.

Life was far from perfect, but it was hers. And with Rishi by her side, she knew she could face whatever challenges lay ahead. Ananya looked at the dandelion, its delicate seeds still intact, and smiled. It wasn't just a weed.

II
The Mirror

Sayan stared at his reflection in the cracked mirror, his eyes tracing the familiar contours of his face. Every day felt like a battle, not just with the world outside, but with the person looking back at him. In his mid-thirties, Sayan had spent most of his life trying to fit into the mold society had cast for him—a cis male, expected to conform to rigid norms of masculinity that felt more like a cage than a comfort.

His phone buzzed on the cluttered counter, breaking the silence of his small apartment. It was a message from his friend Arka.

"Meet up at the bar tonight? Usual place. Need to unwind."

Sayan sighed. The usual place meant loud music, raucous laughter, and the pervasive pressure to act a certain way. He typed a quick reply, "Sure, see you at 8," and tossed the phone aside. He didn't have the energy to explain his feelings, not even to Arka, who had been his friend since college.

Stepping out of his apartment, Sayan walked down the crowded streets of Mumbai, the city's hustle and bustle a constant backdrop to his inner turmoil. He had tried to fit in, to be the man everyone expected him to be—strong, stoic, unflinching. But every time he slipped on that mask, he felt a piece of himself fade away.

At work, he was surrounded by colleagues who embodied the traditional ideals of masculinity. They talked about sports, cars, and women, their conversations often laced with casual misogyny. Sayan had learned to nod along, laughing at the right moments, but it felt hollow, like he was an actor in someone else's play.

The expectations extended to his family, too. His father, a stern man with a rigid sense of duty, often spoke about the importance of being a "real man." His mother, though loving, echoed these sentiments, urging him to settle down, marry, and start a family. Sayan's younger brother, Rahul, seemed to fit the mold effortlessly, excelling in everything from sports to relationships.

As the evening approached, Sayan found himself at the bar, a familiar sense of dread settling in his stomach. He pushed open the heavy door and was greeted by the sound of laughter and the clinking of glasses. Arka waved him over, a wide grin on his face.

"Sayan! Over here!" Arka shouted above the noise.

Sayan forced a smile and made his way to the table. The usual group was there, their faces flushed with alcohol and excitement. They greeted him with hearty slaps on the back and jokes that made him wince inside.

"Hey, Sayan, how's the single life treating you?" one of them teased.

"Living the dream," Sayan replied, his voice flat.

As the night wore on, the conversations grew louder and more boisterous. Sayan found himself drifting, his mind wandering back to the mirror and the reflection that haunted him. He excused himself and stepped outside, the cool night air a welcome relief.

He walked aimlessly, his thoughts a tangled mess. Why was it so hard to be himself? Why did he feel like an imposter in his own skin? The city lights blurred as he wandered through the streets, lost in his own world.

Eventually, he found himself at Marine Drive, the iconic promenade that hugged the coastline. He sat on the concrete embankment, staring out at the dark expanse of the Arabian Sea. The sound of the waves was soothing, a gentle reminder of nature's vastness and his own smallness.

A voice interrupted his thoughts. "Beautiful, isn't it?"

Sayan turned to see an elderly man standing nearby, his face lined with age but his eyes bright with wisdom. He nodded. "Yes, it is."

The man sat down next to him, a comfortable silence settling between them. After a few moments, he spoke again. "You look troubled, my friend."

Sayan sighed. "Just... trying to figure out who I am."

The man nodded, as if he understood. "It's a lifelong journey, finding oneself. The world will always try to tell you who to be, but only you can decide that."

Sayan looked at him, surprised by the depth of his words. "How do you do that? How do you find yourself in a world that doesn't accept you?"

The man smiled. "You start by listening to your own heart, not the voices around you. You embrace the parts of yourself that you've been told to hide. And most importantly, you find your own tribe—people who accept you for who you are."

Sayan felt a weight lift off his shoulders, the man's words resonating deeply. He realized that he had spent too long trying to fit into a mold that was never meant for him. It was time to break free.

As he walked back to his apartment, Sayan felt a renewed sense of purpose. He would start by being honest with himself, embracing the parts of his identity he had suppressed for so long. He would seek out communities where he could be his true self, without fear of judgment.

Back in his apartment, he looked at the cracked mirror one last time. This time, the reflection looking back at him felt different—more authentic, more real. Sayan smiled, a genuine smile that reached his eyes. He was ready to find Sayan.

III

The Dream Catcher

In the depths of a forgotten city, where buildings whispered secrets and shadows danced in eerie patterns, lived the Dream Catcher. She was known by no other name, for her existence transcended ordinary labels. The Dream Catcher resided in a dilapidated tower, its spire reaching towards a sky perpetually cloaked in twilight.

Each night, as the city slumbered, the Dream Catcher embarked on her surreal journey. With a net woven from the threads of moonbeams and stardust, she traversed the realm between dreams and reality. Her task was singular and sacred: to capture fragments of dreams that slipped from the minds of sleepers and weave them into the fabric of existence.

On one particular night, when the moon hung low and stars blinked like distant memories, the Dream Catcher sensed a disturbance in the cosmic tapestry. A dream, unlike any she had encountered, beckoned from the depths of the abyss. Its whispers carried on the wind, weaving through alleys and winding up the tower's staircase.

Intrigued, the Dream Catcher unfurled her net and followed the trail of ethereal whispers. She emerged onto the tower's rooftop, where a figure stood silhouetted against the shimmering skyline. It was a man, clad in a coat of shadows and wearing a mask of forgotten dreams.

"Who are you?" the Dream Catcher asked, her voice a melody that resonated with the night.

The man turned, his eyes, twin pools of starlight. "I am the Echo of Lost Desires," he replied, his voice a haunting echo of distant yearning. "I have wandered these realms seeking solace, seeking release."

The Dream Catcher nodded knowingly. She sensed the weight of his existence, the burden of dreams unfulfilled that draped like heavy cloaks upon his shoulders. Without words, she extended her net towards him, offering to weave his essence into the cosmic fabric.

He hesitated for a moment, then stepped forward into the embrace of moonlit threads. The Dream Catcher worked swiftly, her movements fluid and precise. She captured the Echo's essence, entwining it with the shimmering strands of dreams that danced around them.

As she worked, an elfin rain began to descend on the lips of the night and with each shimmery kiss, he dissipated from her sky.

IV

A Cup of Coffee

His form was unmistakable. He was equally at ease slouching over the railing overlooking the busy city street, as he would have been with a mug of steaming coffee in hand on his favourite armchair.

Every time she looked at him the word that flashed into her head was *relaxed*... not relaxed from life, but he took life as it came with a relaxation that defied human endurance.

Even today, he looked just like that... serene and calm... but definitely not laid-back in the negative sense of the term. Even from a distance, she would not have missed him.

Therefore, there, was no reason to miss him today.

"Sorry I'm late. Have you been waiting very long?" She said it all at one go. He knew she meant it. The consternation of having made him wait was clearly written all over. She looked flustered; somewhat exhausted.

May be the heat, he thought. The mercury levels in the city had been quite unforgiving for a few days now.

"Oh don't worry about that. The traffic can be quite a pain." He had been stuck too. "Let's go somewhere cooler. It's pretty hot out here." Beads of perspiration were lining the edges of his hairline. Something he absolutely hated.

"Yes, that would be a great idea."

They went to the nearest coffee shop although neither actually craved for coffee in the middle of the afternoon. However, such kind of places guaranteed two things.... Working air-conditioning and a table to talk over, and they needed both.

"Know what," she spoke as she winded into the chair, relaxing with the drop in temperature. "Whenever I get into places like these, I can never make up my mind."

"Why? The choices baffle you?" He made a quick decision to discard bringing up the reference of Starbucks from the movie "You've Got Mail". *God that was not even a cult movie. A chick-flick.*

"Oh no. I don't mean like what coffee I want or something like 'You've Got Mail'... *large, medium, small.... cafe/ decafe, with cream/ without.*" She paused to see if her words had registered.

Bummer I should have said it! He felt like saying that aloud. "Ok so no Tom Hanksish dilemma here. So, what are you talking about?" It never failed to amuse him how women liked it when they knew they were understood.

"Well, I can never make up my mind whether to order a cold coffee, which is more appropriate given the fact that I was planning to escape the heat outside or should I settle for something hot to make me feel cosy here, now." She thought for a moment and then added, "You think I am crazy right?"

"Yes... that I most certainly do." He smiled.

She smiled too. She had always been a sport.

Over a latte and a humungous mug of hot chocolate, they picked up the pieces... of times that have been; the time that will be... whatever the other has missed. They were as is fashionably referred to nowadays as *catching up*.

"And hence my friend I have given up on women... I cannot go gaga over anyone anymore and I don't know how else you can tolerate them without that blindfold." He rested his case.

This is what it comes down to then... after endless women, scores of affairs and a couple of real heartbreaks. All it boils down to is resentment, more out of an intellectual deep-freeze than a passionate hatred.

He liked woman only to the extent to which they did not make him feel responsible or smothered. Thus, he liked her. She was just a friend and thankfully, neither of them had ever had any romantic illusions about each other to tarnish that friendship.

"You are being too hard on yourself. You know that. Let it go. Let things work out for you." She hated isolation. After years of being a miserable recluse, she could not imagine anyone wanting to be that. "Nobody is asking you to go out of your way and get that person to settle down with but at least don't take a stance against it too. Let things work out on their own."

Repetition... she repeated her words only when she was perplexed. He laughed aloud to lighten the situation. She of all people should not have minded his decision... but on a second thought maybe she should.

"So, how's everything at your end?" He changed the subject, definitely not because he felt uncomfortable talking about himself. He wanted to know so much about her and time was running out.

"Well... everything is alright." She said with a lazy jerk of her head. Her hair fell all over her face catching the light here and there. She moved it away without any art.

"And how is your guy doing?" they never bothered about names... what was the point of memorising names of love interests when they changed.

She blushed as she spoke. "He's doing fine actually. Haven't talked with him for a few days now because of this vacation, otherwise, the last I heard he was doing great." The blush came in as a rosy tinge. It reminded him of the time when he was in love for the first time. A very soft beginning to what would end up as a whirlwind of distasteful emotional hangover. A melodrama he concluded.

"Last you heard... hmmm..." he mused. "I guess I can safely presume that *last you heard* would not be more than two days."

She reddened. Even to the tip of her nose.

He waited, as he watched her. "So, what, do you really love this guy?" He knew the answer even before he had set the question. He asked her, nevertheless.

Her answer came in laboured halts. "Oh... well ... yes I do." She had had no mind of telling this.

"Does he love you?"

"No, he does not." She said it in the most nonchalant manner, as if it did not matter at all.

"What exactly do you mean?" *Was she completely out of her mind?* She has been going out with this fellow for aeons now. What was she up to?

"You know right... I have told you. He says he cannot love me and all that... blah blah."

"Come on... then why are you still in there? To get more and more hurt."

"Ah... no you don't get it... see I haven't been this happy... ever. I mean it. I am so happy with him."

"But he doesn't love you right? He told you that?" So, my friend has now become a masochist. What a transformation... from an island she goes to become a martyr!

"How can I explain... if you could only see... he cares for me so much more than all those people who claimed to have loved me? I have not been this happy. I wish he could see that too." There was an earnestness in her that clearly stated that she was not making it all up. She meant every word she said, so he did not push it any further.

"What does he think?"

The question was innocuous, but she took her time answering it. "He is infinitely guilty about it all the time. He thinks he is not treating me right."

"Then why don't you let him know?" He rather guessed she must have. He has never known her to leave anything unsaid.

She always spoke out... when she was being abused... when she was being cheated on... she had also spoke out when she was about to commit suicide. Reticence was one thing his friend never had... absence of that one quality assured his friend's presence by his side today.

"I tell him that all the time. I guess he thinks I say all that to make him feel better."

"Then you are in for some circumlocution, aren't you?" Thankfully, the problem was not as great as he had hunched it to be. However, he thought he might just test the waters further. "Ok, what happens when he goes away?"

The question left her shell-shocked. The espresso she had ordered next faced the imminent danger of lying there on the table cold and untouched. Therefore, he spoke up, "I asked only hypothetically."

"The thing is... I have been thinking about this a lot. Guess it all boils down to the fact that if he leaves me, I would just have to get used to it... adjust and start living again." She looked controlled. However, the very thought of separation had scared the wits out of her... it was plain for everyone to see... naturally so did he.

"You won't be able to, you know that." He gave her a hard look. "I might be able to lead a life completely walled off. I might even end up enjoying my solitude, muse my loneliness. I am after all the proverbial introvert. You on the other hand would just fall apart." He had never meant to tell her this. It was in a way insulting, but when he had begun, it seemed like foolhardy to stop without saying everything. "I wouldn't wish for you to suffer anymore.

You will not be able to take it. Not after all those miserable years. If this guy has made you so happy, I pray to God he stays because I shudder to imagine what you will be like once he's not there."

Repetition… was that not a sign of perplexity?

She kept quiet for a while. A film of moisture was glistening in her eyes. She deftly whisked it away using the pretext of arranging her hair. "Let's be optimistic." She was lying through her teeth. "He wouldn't go. I know… I mean I hope he would not. And even if he does, I have friends like you to fall back on, right?"

"Yeah right." He let in a sigh. *He hoped she was right. He hoped he was enough to see her through.*

"Gosh. It is four already. I have to leave. See you sometime later and hey thanks for talking." She did not want to stay any longer. She had said it as plainly as possible.

"Oh yes absolutely. See you." He did not ask her to stay back. She would not have had even if he did. She had not come here looking for sympathy or help. She had just come to share a cup of coffee with an old friend in the city.

She left without tarrying any further. She paid for the coffee and made a dash.

Getting out of the coffee shop, he landed on a sidewalk teeming with people. She would be here somewhere, he thought, making her way towards her car.

Then he saw her… a small head bobbing up and down. Her confident yet speedy gait a dead give-away.

Her form was unmistakable to him. Even from a distance, he could not have missed her.

She would be crying once she was inside the car. This was something he knew. Was not that what friends did… they knew you… even if you thought they did not?

He smiled to himself as a prayer issued from his lips. He hoped for it to be answered.

He turned around and started walking the other way in search of his car. He had a home to go back too.

V
Cinderella Once Again

The early morning mist clung to the branches like a reluctant lover lingering the embrace before the final moment of departure. The damp stretch of concrete was awakened by the caressing feet of joggers. The birds were slowly arising from their aerial dreams...

The dew drenched park donned the freshness of a young damsel just visited by adolescence. Sauntering down the leaf laden path I looked up to find the nascent rays peeping through the dark edges of the horizon.... The sky appeared like a new bride, all rosy and flushed after a night of brimming intoxication and melting surrender.

I drank in the moist green with my roving eyes...and as the path came to a sharp bend, I saw her!!! The surrounding trees screened her from public view yet her once majestic form was unmistakable. She was seated on a deserted bench, draped in faded brocade that whispered tales of once upon a time opulence. She sat with her chin almost caressing her neckline. Eyes downcast, crossed hands loosely resting on her lap.

I tiptoed to the spot exercising extreme caution not to break her reverie. I stood there for some time, but she seemed to have made "oblivion" her lone watchword...nothing seemed to perturb her!!! Suddenly to my consternation she lifted her pale face, a face redolent of a bygone impeccable beauty. The once marble smooth complexion now wan, wrinkles lurked around the corner of a Michelangelesque sculpted mouth. Dark half-moons cast their shadows under her weary eyes.

Before I could frame my query, her silence impressed these words upon my mind…” I'm your beloved city. I have long bidden farewell to my halcyon days…have travelled down the highways of time…history reduced me from riches to rags. Over and over again my modesty has been outraged. Society has walked over my soul. But I had my days of glory too, when the sun shone brightly…. I long for my lost grandeur…I walk the streets of torment like a spectre doomed forever….my chariot has vanished…my slippers broken…. can you weave your magic? Can you make me Cinderella once again?”

VI
The Hoarder

Deep within the cluttered apartment of Sameer stood a mountain of possessions, each item layered in dust and memories. The air was thick with a musty scent, a testament to years of accumulation. Sameer navigated the narrow paths he had carved through his belongings, each step a journey through his past.

The faded photograph of his parents' wedding, tucked under a stack of old newspapers, caught his eye. Sameer picked it up gently, brushing off the dust. He could almost hear his mother's laughter and his father's deep voice, vibrant and alive in the sepia tones. This photograph wasn't just paper; it was a portal to a time when he felt loved and secure.

He moved to the bookshelf, its shelves sagging under the weight of countless books. Each book had a story beyond its pages. The worn copy of "The Wuthering Heights" his sister had gifted him before she moved abroad, a gesture of their shared love for literature. He hadn't seen her in years, but the book kept her presence alive in his world.

Sameer's gaze shifted to a cracked teacup, its delicate handle missing. It was part of a set his wife had brought into their marriage. She had left him a decade ago, unable to live in the growing chaos, but the teacup remained, a symbol of the life they once shared. Holding it, he could almost hear the clinking of cups and their whispered conversations during quiet afternoons.

The clock on the wall, its hands frozen at 3:15, was a relic from his childhood home. Sameer remembered the day it stopped, coinciding with the moment his father had passed away. The clock's silence mirrored the void left in his life. It was a constant reminder of loss, but also of the love that had once filled their home.

Every item in Sameer's apartment was a piece of his history. They were not just objects; they were fragments of his identity, each holding a piece of his heart. Letting go of even one would feel like losing a part of himself, a part of his story.

The doorbell rang, pulling Sameer out of his trance. It was his friend, Susmit, the only person who still visited him. Susmit stepped carefully through the maze of belongings, his face a mix of concern and resignation.

"Sameer, we need to talk," Susmit began gently. "This... this isn't healthy. You can't keep living like this."

Sameer sighed, his eyes scanning the room. "I know it looks bad, but these things... they're all I have left. Each one means something to me."

Susmit nodded, understanding the pain in Sameer's voice. "I get it, but you're burying yourself in memories. You need space to create new ones, to live."

Sameer's eyes welled up. He knew Susmit was right, but the thought of parting with his belongings was unbearable. "It's not that simple, Susmit. These things are my life."

Susmit placed a hand on Sameer's shoulder. "Then let's take it one step at a time. Start with something small. We'll do it together."

Sameer hesitated, then nodded slowly. He picked up an old magazine, the pages yellowed with age. It was a start, a tiny step towards reclaiming his life. He placed it in a carton Susmit held out, feeling a pang of loss but also a glimmer of hope.

As Susmit replaced the flaps of the cardboard carton, Sameer broke into uncontrollable sobs. The pretty face of his mother emerged from the pile of ashes after the fire inside the incinerator had nothing to burn.

VII

The Shadow Within

Amit sat alone in the dimly lit apartment, the weight of his decisions bearing down on him like a leaden sky. The flickering glow of his laptop screen cast shadows that danced across his face, mirroring the turmoil within. His hands trembled as he scrolled through emails filled with pleas from fellow activists, reminders of the battles they fought together, and the ideals they held dear.

He had been a stalwart defender of the environment, a crusader against corporate greed and environmental destruction. His convictions had fuelled protests, inspired articles that exposed deceit, and rallied a community around a shared cause. But tonight, exhaustion and disillusionment clawed at him like never before.

After a gruelling protest that ended in violence, Amit returned home drained and defeated. He sank into his chair and stared blankly at the laptop screen. A targeted advertisement flashed at the corner—a slick promotion from a major oil company, boasting of its commitment to sustainability. It was a facade he had debunked countless times, but tonight, something stirred deep within him—a whisper of doubt, a seed of compromise.

Against his better judgment, Amit clicked on the link.

The company's website dazzled with promises of innovation and environmental stewardship. Photos of smiling faces and pristine landscapes mocked him, each image a calculated deception designed to mollify public outrage and justify profit. Despite his rising anger, a part of him was intrigued—a dangerous allure of compromise whispered seductively, tempting him with the prospect of making a difference from within.

Days turned into weeks as Amit found himself entangled in negotiations with the very industry he had vowed to oppose. Meetings in corporate boardrooms replaced street protests. His inbox overflowed with invitations to industry events where he was hailed as a visionary collaborator—a title that tasted bitter on his tongue.

Guilt gnawed at him relentlessly, a constant companion as he navigated murky waters of compromise and concession. He avoided the accusing glances of fellow activists, unable to meet their eyes knowing he had betrayed their trust and his own principles. Yet, he justified his actions as necessary steps towards achieving tangible results, a bitter pill swallowed in the name of progress.

One stormy night, rain hammered against the windowpanes of his apartment, a relentless rhythm that mirrored the turmoil in Amit's soul. Alone in the shadowy embrace of his thoughts, he retrieved a worn journal from a forgotten drawer—a journal filled with fervent declarations and unwavering convictions that now felt like distant echoes of a past life.

Tears welled in his eyes as he confronted the stark truth—he had betrayed himself. The ideals that once burned fiercely within him had dimmed to embers, suffocated by compromise and expediency. With trembling hands, he drafted a resignation letter to the company, a defiant act of reclaiming his integrity and confronting the consequences of his choices.

As he pressed send, a sense of liberation surged through him—a bitter yet cathartic release from the chains of compromise. The storm outside intensified, unleashing a torrential downpour that washed away the dust.

VIII
Distant Echoes

...She felt the brush of lips on her earlobe as she opened her languid eyes. The serenade of the previous night floated back in prismatic slices, conjured by the kaleidoscope of her bleary mind.

Too weary to look around, she stretched her slender leg to encounter her negligee sulking beneath her feet. She rummaged through her mind, but all she felt were waves of Lethe lapping at the edges of her memory.

Invisible fingers had left their imprints all over her flesh. The chromatic resplendence was vivid, yet the face remained blurred. Was her subconscious playing havoc? Was he there, or was it a figment of her imagination? Had she stumbled into a time warp? Each query flapped its wings in vain like an ineffectual angel.

In the remote crevices of her mind, wispy images of a long-forgotten face danced—distant but uncannily familiar, fleeting yet indelible.

The penumbra of appearance and reality escorted the veil of somnolence. Slowly, she draped herself in the misty anticipation of being cradled in those arms, so familiar yet so forgotten.

IX
Emancipation

In the heart of an ancient city, where time-worn cobblestones whispered secrets beneath hurried feet, a man named Azaad moved with a sense of purpose. The narrow alleyways twisted and turned, guiding him through the labyrinthine streets. Azaad was a man of many faces, known to some as a scholar, to others as a ghost. But today, his mission was dark, his heart heavy with the weight of what he had vowed to do.

Azaad had once been a poet, a lover of words and dreams. But the ravages of war had torn his world apart, leaving him a hollow shell. In his despair, he had been drawn into a group that promised vengeance and justice. They had filled his heart with rage and his mind with the cold determination of a soldier. His poetry books had been replaced by weapons, his dreams by a singular, destructive purpose.

As he walked through the bustling market, the scent of spices and the vibrant colors of the stalls stirred memories of a life he had lost. His hand brushed against the concealed device beneath his coat, a stark reminder of the path he had chosen. He had been tasked with a mission that would bring chaos to the city, a mission he believed would avenge the wrongs done to his people.

But as Azaad approached the crowded square, something inexplicable happened. A strange light, almost imperceptible, began to emanate from the amulet he wore around his neck. The amulet was an heirloom, given to him by his grandmother, who had whispered tales of its protective powers and mystical origins. It was said to hold the spirit of a guardian who watched over their family.

The light grew stronger, enveloping Azaad in a warm, golden glow. He stopped, his breath catching in his throat, as a figure materialized before him. She was ethereal, her form shimmering with a radiant energy. Her eyes, deep and knowing, met his with an intensity that pierced through the fog of his anger.

"Azaad," she spoke, her voice a balmy tone that echoed in his mind. "You carry a burden that is not yours to bear. Your heart is not made for hatred, but for love and creation. Remember who you are."

Azaad trembled, the weight of her words crashing over him. Images of his past life flooded his mind—the joy of writing, the warmth of his family's embrace, the beauty of a world seen through the eyes of a poet. Tears streamed down his face as he realized how far he had strayed from the path he was meant to walk.

The guardian extended her hand, and Azaad felt a profound sense of peace wash over him. The device beneath his coat seemed to grow heavier, a symbol of the darkness he was ready to cast aside. With a trembling hand, he removed it, placing it on the ground at her feet.

"Choose life, Azaad," she whispered. "Choose love and hope."

As the light around her began to fade, Azaad felt a renewed sense of purpose. He turned away from the square, leaving the device behind, and walked back through the market. The colors seemed brighter, the scents richer, and the sounds more vibrant. He was a poet once more, a dreamer in a world that needed his light.

The city continued to buzz with life, unaware of the disaster that had been averted. In the heart of the ancient city, a new journey began, one that would be written with the ink of redemption and the quill of love.

A distant shot shattered the silence, striking deep into the poet's heart, the one who dreamt of crafting verses 'recollected in blood and fire.' Blood spurted and splattered on the cold cobblestones, as Qaisar's lines flashed through his fading vision: 'jigar ka khoon bhi kuchh chahiye asar ke liye.'

'Recollected in blood and fire,'

X
Dream Dust

The rain was on its last bout of sobs when she stepped out of the tall brown building.... the smell of sodden earth filled her nostrils slowly carving a way to her mind.... the sky looked down wistfully with tear-stained eyes...there was a strange sadness .... suddenly the magic butterflies stopped fluttering their wings inside her heart....

The euphoria that had captivated her in its thraldom for the past few days was gradually dissipating...Oh no! She could hear the hoof beats of those riders of Apocalypse once again...why do they always appear when the lady of Shallot sits in front of her magic mirror.... hasn't the mirror cracked for a zillion times???

She frantically groped for those unburnt logs that she had stashed somewhere in the secret dungeons of her mind...those logs must be set ablaze before the riders reach their destination.... the chill was slowly creeping in.... soon everything would get frozen.... Her mind recalled, "Where are the songs of spring...aye where are they...?" The grey rider whispered..." they will never be sung again......the choristers have all departed.... the magician has vanished once again...."

She woke up with a start...the tiny specks of yet another shattered dream floated all around her crystal maze of loneliness......

XI
An Apocalyptic Christmas

He had grown to loneliness as creepers grow on deserted mansions—since his retirement, his first stroke, and since she departed. The years had applied coats of reticence over him, like dark painted nails in a beauty magazine. But in his case, the enamel wouldn't flake off. She loved to paint her nails. He gazed wistfully at the array of bottles on the dressing table—some empty, some half-filled. The dried varnish, once red, orange, purple, pink, now black... all the different shades of pain.

Loving her was like a day in autumn— 'mists and mellow fruitfulness.' He prided on their ripe love but dreaded the inevitable consequence. Didn't they say, 'ripeness is all'? But nothing could enervate their love, not even death. It was still throbbing and young. She died at the age of 33, the very age when *love* itself died, he reflected, but in her case, it wasn't on a couple of intersected wooden beams. She would have been 68 this winter, but death had eternalized her age. Forever thirty-three, forever young, beautiful, and steadfast to this septuagenarian widower.

When he married her, she was so young and delicate that he was afraid to touch her. Those dark, innocent eyes gave his heart a tug whenever he gazed into them. Then the fear of losing her would wash over him, anesthetizing him until he congregated all his might to chide himself out of his apoplexy. Strangely enough, that fear of loss had died with her. For those ten years of marital life, his entire being was so full of her thoughts that no other thing seemed to have any existence. And after ten brief years of pure, crystalline bliss, he suddenly found himself at the dead end of the road. Living without her was an anathema. But what had he done to incite the wrath of the Gods?

He had tried to possess her—body and soul. Was that his tragic flaw? But what else could he have done? Not that there was a dearth of pretty girls in the college—some would have scaled risky heights to trek the path of life with him. And why not? He had a promising future ahead... But he just couldn't summon enough courage. Shyness, perhaps, was his tragic error. He was nicknamed Michelangelo by his classmates for his indifference to the opposite sex, but he endured their sneers without any flutter. He had pledged to lavish on his wife all his love, and he had lived up to that self-commitment. After her death, he was pestered by friends and relatives to tie the knot again. It was blasphemous! Didn't they know he was wedded to her love for the rest of his life?

Occasionally, when his friends paid visits, she played the perfect hostess, maintaining a subtle aloofness. That impressed him very much. Today there's no shame in confessing that whenever a certain friend paid particular attention to her, he felt jealous. But isn't jealousy an ingredient of love? There was this friend—whom she nicknamed Lucifer—who particularly adored her. She felt he was 'needlessly friendly.' It gave him unspeakable pleasure to see Lucifer make advances and retreat crestfallen. The setting was perfectly Biblical, but the act of temptation would never be fruitful. Nothing could beguile his Eve. Their paradise would never be lost. He sometimes wondered, 'What do I have in me to make her ignore handsome guys like Lucifer?' Perhaps it was pure love and devotion. She was hopelessly devoted to him. Hopelessly attached. The very thought of being separated from her was death.

Throughout that thrilling decade, he was compelled to stay away from her only on three occasions—once, when he had to be away on an official tour to Jaipur. Those three days seemed like three deserts he had to cross on foot. Then, when she miscarried and had to remain in the hospital for a week, he would give anything to forget that trauma. The fatal infection following the miscarriage effected the final separation. Would it ever end? A mild rumbling of thunder hauled him out of his memories. A fine drizzle began to descend on the dry ground. Brumal rain. How she loved it! The raindrops playfully drummed on the eaves and turned the panes hazy. But why did his glasses get hazy... hasn't he left spring far behind?

Involuntarily, he rose from the easy-chair and walked towards her cupboard. He had not opened it since she left. He said a little prayer as he stood before it. He could do nothing to stop the trembling of his hands as he removed the piles of neatly folded clothes, to retrieve the album that treasured her photographs. Where could she have tucked it away? Since her death, he had not needed to open the album. She was always there on his mind, smiling, pouting, whispering sweet nothings. Why was he looking for it today? Senile whims...

Suddenly, his fingers touched something hard beneath a pile of woollen clothes. He carefully removed the pile—it was a beautiful rosewood box with exquisite carvings—the gift he had brought for her from Jaipur. His hands trembled so violently that it necessitated all his gripping power. Slowly he staggered towards the bed with the box held close to his heart. He couldn't tell for how long he sat undecided on the bed with the box held tightly in his hands.

Finally, with a Herculean effort, he lifted the lid. It was like resurrecting the past that had been buried for thirty-five long years. There were trinkets—a few pairs of earrings, rings, a gold chain with a heart-shaped locket. He had never seen her wearing this chain; but then she had so many of these that it was hard to remember. As he touched the purple velvet handkerchief on which the jewellery rested, the blood in his veins seemed to ripple. It was like caressing her face after so many years. He softly lifted the square piece of velvet. And it was then his eyes came to rest on the envelope that was concealed beneath—no! There were two envelopes. With jittery fingers, he brought out the sheet of paper from the first one. It was dated the tenth of April, a week prior to his departure to Jaipur:

Dearest M,

It seems incredible. Just another week to go and you would be mine for three whole days and nights. The mere thought of it sets my blood on fire. I promise you'll receive your much-awaited gift this time.

Yours ever,
Lucifer.

It's a pity the great master spoke so unfairly of the fair sex.

The next letter was written on the 23rd of September, a fortnight after her miscarriage:

Dearest M,

I'm terribly shocked at the news. How could you be so careless to lose my baby just like that? But then you could call it a blessing in disguise. Had the child lived, it could never have had the privilege to call me 'father'…

Nothing could beguile his Eve. Their paradise would never be lost.

The rest was blurred. Blankly, he replaced the letters in the box, stood up, and walked steadily across to the corner where the dressing table stood. She loved to paint her nails. She was hopelessly devoted to him.

"Needlessly friendly."

"My baby…"

Stupefied, he picked up the shabby bottles and threw them one by one out of the window. A tide of nausea swept across his entire system, making him turn sharply to grip the bedpost for support. As he began to slump on the floor, his eyes caught those magical numbers on the date calendar resting on the table… 25… December 25… Christmas was being celebrated all over the world… but love was dead long ago.

XII

The Arrival

The snowflakes descended like an august requiem.... she pressed her nose to the glass pane to watch the brumal whim... her warm breath creating circular patterns on the glass blurring the vision...a desperate attempt to ward off the chill that was gradually creeping in through the shadows of her mind....

A stray black cat sauntered along the white driveway brindled by the naughty snowflakes...did it know where it was heading for.... why was she standing there? Oblivion twirled around the room in small circles....

The logs in the fireplace wistfully awaited that fiery embrace but Boreas had left his footprints everywhere.... somewhere in the bower of Titania, Zephyrus played his panpipe under the canopy of blue bells and cowslips.... inside this frozen cave her soul lay under the piano like a cramped scroll...too brittle to be unfurled....

......the snail was crawling at a zero speed.... did the snow- dappled feline reach its destination....??? There was a smothered knock on the door.... the crone has finally arrived....

XIII

Departure

Amidst a small, sunlit garden, there stood an ancient oak tree. Its branches stretched wide, offering shade and shelter to all who came near. Beside the oak, nestled in the soft earth, was a delicate lilac bush. Its blossoms were a vibrant lilac, standing in stark contrast to Oak's rugged bark. There was one special lilac that tugged a cord in the oak's rough bosom whenever the gentle breeze blew over the bush. This one particular lilac swayed with such grace that it sent shivers down his jagged bark.

From the moment the lilac bush sprouted, the oak felt a deep connection. He admired her beauty and the way her petals caught the morning dew. the blossom, in turn, looked up to Oak's sturdy presence, feeling protected under his vast canopy.

Seasons changed, and their bond grew stronger. When the sun blazed harshly, he would stretch his leaves to cast a cooling shadow over his delicate beloved, protecting her from the scorching rays. In return, the lilac's fragrance filled the air, attracting bees that pollinated the oak's acorns, ensuring the continuation of his lineage.

One autumn, a fierce storm swept through the garden. Winds howled, and an unforgiving rain battered the earth. The oak felt his branches groan under the pressure, but his concern was for the lilac. He braced himself against the storm, his roots digging deeper to hold firm. The next morning, as the storm clouds cleared, he looked down and to his consternation found the bush missing from its place. He stretched his branches, frantically seeking the lilac. Tears started to stream down his woody cheeks, soaking the withered lilac that lay lifeless in a crevice at his foot.

XIV
Stasis

Cradled in the lap of Chandrapur stood an old clock tower, its hands frozen in time. The clock had stopped at precisely 3:47 PM many years ago, yet it remained a beloved fixture in the small-town square. The townspeople often joked that while the clock no longer kept time, it kept their stories.

On a crisp autumn morning, Mrs. Harman, the town historian, made her daily visit to the clock tower. She ran her fingers along its weathered face, a habit she had developed over the years. "If only you could talk," she whispered. "Imagine the tales you'd tell."

Unbeknownst to her, the clock did remember. Though its hands were immobile, its gears and springs held the memories of Chandrapur's inhabitants.

Decades ago, at exactly 3:47 PM, young Ishan had knelt under this very clock to propose to Ayushi. Ayushi's laughter, sparkling like sunlight, had filled the square as she said yes. That moment of joy was etched into the clock's silent heart.

On a rainy afternoon ten years later, the clock had witnessed a different scene. Mohan Singh had stood beneath it, holding a telegram that shattered his world. His only son, fighting in a distant war, had fallen in battle. The sorrow of that moment seeped into the clock's mechanisms, a poignant counterpoint to Ishan and Ayushi's happiness.

Years passed, and the clock tower stood sentinel over the town's unfolding stories. Children played in its shadow, lovers carved their initials into its base, and old friends met beneath its steady gaze. It became a silent witness to life's ebb and flow, each event adding another layer to its silent chronicle.

One spring day, a stranger arrived in Chandrapur. Tall and gaunt, with a sombre expression, he carried a toolbox and a curious glint in his eye. He introduced himself as Ilias, a clockmaker. Word spread quickly, and soon a crowd gathered around the clock tower.

"I've heard about your broken clock," Ilias said, addressing the townspeople. "I'd like to fix it."

Murmurs of excitement and scepticism rippled through the crowd. The clock had been frozen for so long that many had come to see its stopped hands as a symbol of their town's enduring spirit. But curiosity won out, and they agreed to let Elias try.

For days, Ilias worked tirelessly, climbing the rickety ladder to the clock's inner workings. He dismantled its parts, each piece a puzzle revealing the town's history. As he worked, he listened to the townspeople's stories about the clock, piecing together the narrative of Chandrapur.

One afternoon, Mrs. Harman visited Ilias at the clock tower. "You've been working so hard," she said, offering him a cup of tea. "What drives you to fix our old clock?"

Ilias paused, gazing at the motionless hands. "I believe every clock has a soul," he replied. "Yours is filled with the memories of this town. By repairing it, I hope to honour those memories and give new life to them."

Mrs. Harman nodded, touched by his words. She left him to his work, feeling a renewed sense of hope for the old clock.

Finally, the day came when Ilias was ready to restart the clock. The townspeople gathered, holding their breath as he wound the mechanism. With a creak and a groan, the hands began to move. The clock chimed, its sound reverberating through the square like a heartbeat.

As the clock resumed its rhythm, something magical happened. The townspeople felt a rush of memories, as if the clock were sharing its tales. They saw Ishan and Ayushi's joyful proposal, felt the weight of Mohan Singhs' grief, and relived countless other moments that had shaped their lives.

Tears filled their eyes as they realized the clock had been more than a timekeeper; it had been a guardian of their collective history. Now, with its hands moving once more, it promised to continue holding their stories for generations to come.

Ilias stood back, watching the townspeople embrace their rekindled connection to the past. Mrs. Harman approached him, a smile on her face. "Thank you, Ilias," she said. "You've given us more than just a working clock. You've given us our memories."

Ilias nodded; his heart full. "Time moves forward," he said softly, "but it's the moments we remember that give it meaning."

XV

The Embrace

In the quiet stillness of a moonlit night, Solitude and Loneliness found themselves drawn together in an ethereal realm where words were whispered on the breath of the wind.

Solitude, cloaked in a serene aura of introspection and tranquillity, stood amidst a tranquil forest clearing. The air was crisp with the scent of pine and earth, the only sound the gentle rustle of leaves in the breeze. Loneliness, draped in shadows that seemed to flicker and dance with melancholy, approached cautiously from the edge of the clearing, a hesitant figure cloaked in uncertainty.

Solitude greeted Loneliness with a gentle smile, her eyes reflecting the wisdom of ages spent in quiet contemplation. "Welcome," she murmured softly, her voice a soothing melody that echoed through the stillness. "I sensed your presence, drifting on the edges of the night."

Loneliness hesitated, uncertain of her reception. "I... I didn't mean to intrude," she replied, her voice tinged with a delicate sorrow. "I have wandered these paths alone for so long, lost in the labyrinth of my own thoughts."

Solitude shook her head gently, understanding etched in the lines of her face. "You are not an intruder here," she assured Loneliness. "In me, there is space for all emotions to unfold, even those as tender and fragile as yours."

Loneliness looked around the clearing, her gaze lingering on the tranquil beauty that surrounded them. "I envy your peace," she admitted quietly. "In the depths of my existence, there is only emptiness, an ache that echoes in the caverns of my heart."

Solitude approached Loneliness with a graceful step, her presence a gentle embrace that offered comfort without words. "Loneliness," she murmured, her voice a whisper of understanding, "you are not defined by your emptiness. Within you lies a depth of feeling, a yearning for connection that mirrors the human experience."

Loneliness trembled, touched by Solitude's compassion. "But how do I find solace in this solitude?" she asked, her voice trembling with vulnerability. "Every path I tread seems to lead back to the ache of isolation."

Solitude nodded thoughtfully, her eyes gazing into the depths of Loneliness's soul. "Solitude is not the absence of others," she explained gently. "It is the presence of oneself, a sanctuary where introspection becomes a journey of self-discovery. Embrace the silence, for within it lies the whispers of your own truth."

Loneliness listened intently, her heart opening to the wisdom woven in Solitude's words. "And what of the yearning for companionship?" she ventured; her voice hesitant yet hopeful. "Is there room for that within the sanctuary of solitude?"

Solitude smiled knowingly, her gaze turning towards the starlit sky above. "Yes," she replied softly. "I teach hearts to cherish the connections that enrich lives, to savour the moments of shared laughter and shared tears. It is in me that people learn to love themselves deeply, so that they may love others authentically."

Loneliness sighed, a weight, lifting from her shoulders as she embraced the understanding unfolding within her. "I have feared myself for so long," she confessed, her voice filled with quiet wonder. "But perhaps I am not my enemy, but a companion on this journey of self-discovery."

Solitude nodded in agreement, her presence a beacon of acceptance and grace. "Indeed," she murmured, "you and I are intertwined threads in the tapestry of our lives. Embrace both with an open heart, and you will find that they can coexist harmoniously, guiding you towards a deeper understanding of yourself and the world around you."

The moon cast a silver glow over the clearing, a timeless witness to the conversation unfolding between Solitude and Loneliness. In that quiet sanctuary, they stood together—two figures united in the fragile dance of human experience, bound by the delicate balance of solitude's embrace and loneliness's longing.

And as the night deepened and stars blinked in silent contemplation, Solitude and Loneliness found solace in each other's presence, discovering that within the depths of solitude lay the seed of connection, and within the ache of loneliness bloomed the possibility of profound self-discovery.

In the embrace of one's wisdom and the other's vulnerability, they found a sacred communion—a touchy and captivating dialogue that echoed through the ages, whispering to all who wandered the paths of solitude and sought solace in the depths of their own hearts.

XVI
An Insignificant Farewell

On a sunlit meadow, now a rare and shrinking sanctuary amidst the encroaching concrete, an elderly buffalo named Bhima lay on the cool grass. His coat, once sleek and strong, was now marked with patches of gray, a testament to the years he had witnessed and the changes he had endured.

Bhima chewed slowly on the sparse grass, his gaze wandering over the horizon where the skyline of the nearby city loomed ominously. Towers of glass and steel rose where fields and forests once flourished. He sighed; a deep, resonant sound that echoed with memories of a world now almost forgotten.

In his youth, the countryside had been a sprawling canvas of green, dotted with vibrant wildflowers and flowing streams. He remembered the joy of roaming freely, the thrill of feeling the earth beneath his hooves as he and his herd grazed on lush pastures that stretched as far as the eye could see. The air had been fresh and filled with the songs of birds and the rustling of leaves. Life had been simple, rhythmic, and harmonious with nature's cycles.

Now, the landscape was fragmented by roads and encircled by fences, the fields broken apart by the relentless advance of urbanization. The streams had dried up, and the birdsong had been replaced by the hum of machinery and the distant roar of traffic. The once-abundant grass was sparse and brittle, and the wildflowers had long since disappeared, their colors replaced by the dull gray of pavement and construction sites.

Bhima's mind drifted back to the farmers who had cared for him and his herd. They were kind and respectful, understanding the bond between land and livestock. The farmers had worked the soil with their hands, planting crops and tending to the animals with a sense of duty and reverence. Now, those farmers were fewer, their fields sold to developers, their livelihoods uprooted like the very soil they once nurtured.

The buffalo's rumination was interrupted by a distant clatter of construction. He turned his head slowly, watching as yet another swath of land was cleared for a new housing complex. The scent of freshly turned earth, mixed with the acrid smell of machinery, wafted over the meadow, a stark contrast to the sweet, natural aromas of the past.

As the sun began to set, casting a golden glow over the encroaching cityscape, Bhima felt a profound sadness. He was one of the last of his herd, many having succumbed to the pressures of a changing world. The younger buffaloes, those who had never known the boundless fields of his youth, adapted to the new reality, but Bhima could not forget.

In the quiet twilight, Bhima lay down on the grass, his body heavy with the weight of memories. He knew his days were numbered, and soon, the meadow itself might vanish, claimed by the relentless spread of urban sprawl. But in his heart, he carried the essence of the past, the spirit of a time when the earth was generous, and life was in balance.

Bhima closed his eyes, allowing the soft whispers of the wind to lull him into a peaceful sleep. He dreamed of endless green fields, of freedom and abundance, a world where the concrete jungle was but a distant nightmare. In his final moments, he found solace in these memories, his legacy woven into the fabric of the land he loved.

As the stars began to emerge, one by one, Bhima breathed his last, becoming part of the earth once more. The meadow remained, for now, a silent testament to what once was, and a reminder of what had been lost.

XVII
The Tears of Ouranos

The sky cried itself to sleep last night. Who knew there were so many tears in his eyes?

After Nox bade adieu to the tear-stained horizon, Aurora arrived in her grey chariot, bumping along the warty surface of the stretch of gloom. The puddles on either side appeared venomous blue.

Millions of light years below, a lonely planet spun its destiny with the wispy gossamer of unrequited dreams. The sky had once promised to share its rainbow. That promise, she reminisced wistfully, lay buried beneath the sands of oblivion.

From the casement of his colossal bower, the sky cast his gaze downward with puffy eyes. Far below, in a deserted corner, the lonely planet sat on her revolving chair, locked in the arms of Somnus. Her closed eyes desperately tried to hold back the dream with her imprisoning long lashes. The spindle shivered in her delicate hands.

Eternity above, a sigh escaped from a pair of moist lips that tasted of salt. If only she knew the night before, he had shed all his tears to plant the rainbow outside her window she had left open for eons. But she had shifted an orbit. Somnolence had sealed her eyes with his silken kiss.

XVIII
The Threshold

The walls of my study have begun to whisper. At first, I dismissed it as the creaking of an old house, the settling of wood and plaster. But now, the whispers form words, sentences, mocking me with the stories I'm yet to write, the characters I've failed to bring to life.

Each morning, I sit at my desk, quill in hand, ink bottle poised, and stare at the blank parchment. The stories used to flow effortlessly, a torrent of creativity that filled pages with worlds and lives. But now, the ink has dried up, replaced by an empty void that mocks me with its silence.

Yesterday, I found myself talking back to the whispers, pleading with them to leave me in peace. My reflection in the window—a gaunt, haggard version of myself—watched with pity. "You're losing your mind," it seemed to say, its eyes mirroring the chaos within me.

My publisher's letters pile up, unopened. I know what they contain: deadlines, expectations, disappointment. I imagine their faces, furrowed brows and pursed lips, questioning why their once-prolific author has become a shadow of his former self.

Last night, the whispers grew louder, insistent. "Write," they commanded. "Write or be forgotten." Desperation clawed at my mind, and I scribbled furiously, words tumbling onto the page in a frantic, incoherent scrawl. When I looked at what I had written, it made no sense—a jumble of thoughts, half-formed ideas, and a haunting refrain: "The story is within you, but you have lost the key."

The quill trembles in my hand, the ink, a pool of mist. I must write, I must find the key. But as the whispers grow louder, more insistent, I wonder if the key is lost forever, and with it, my name but what is my name?

XIX

The Swan Song

In the twilight of an era scarred by human hubris, the last Iron Birch stood sentinel. Its ancient bark, weathered and worn, bore witness to epochs of prosperity and ruin, a silent observer of humanity's ascent and descent. The Tree's gnarled branches stretched towards a darkened sky, once verdant leaves now brittle and yellowed, whispering secrets of a world lost to neglect.

Amidst a landscape ravaged by unchecked progress and ecological upheaval, a disparate group gathered beneath the Tree's fading canopy. They came not as individuals but as embodiments of disparate cultures and ideologies, united by a shared lament for what had been and a fragile hope for redemption.

In the quietude of their gathering, the birch stirred, its essence resonating through the air in a subtle symphony of rustling leaves and whispered echoes. The assembled listeners, attuned to the Tree's silent plea, felt a stirring within their souls—a recognition of their interconnectedness with the natural world and a solemn acknowledgment of their collective culpability in its decline.

The Tree's message unfurled like tendrils of mist weaving through their thoughts:

"I am the last vestige of an ancient covenant between Earth and humanity, a witness to the rise and fall of civilizations, and the custodian of forgotten wisdom. My roots delve deep into the soil, drawing sustenance from the

Earth's core and channelling the pulse of life through my weathered limbs.

"In the twilight of my existence, I beseech you to remember. Remember the forests that once carpeted these lands, teeming with biodiversity and whispers of centuries past. Remember the rivers and streams, once pristine veins coursing through the Earth's veins, now choked by debris and indifference.

"You have forsaken the balance that sustains all life, viewing nature not as kin but as a resource to be exploited for fleeting gain. Your industries have scarred the land, your progress has poisoned the air, and your apathy has severed the threads that bind you to the Earth's rhythm.

"Yet, in the waning breaths of my existence, I implore you to awaken. Let my plight be a testament to the consequences of neglect and the resilience of life's spirit.

In the fading light of a world on the brink, the last sylvan's message hung heavy in the air, a lament for a planet teetering on the edge of oblivion. The gathered souls, burdened by the weight of their own complicity, dispersed into the ashen landscape, their footsteps echoing hollowly against the barren earth.

XX

The Longing

They coexisted where the boundaries of time blurred, beyond human sight. She was a radiant figure, adorned with the colors of dawn, vibrant and ever-changing. Her laughter was the melody of birds, her breath the rustle of leaves, and her touch the warmth of the sun. He, on the other hand, was a solemn presence, cloaked in the midnight shades of black and silver. His voice was the whisper of the wind, his gaze the stillness of night, and his touch the quiet release from suffering.

They were destined to dance around each other for eternity, but never to meet. She adored him from afar, her heart yearning for his calm and serenity. She saw in him the promise of rest after the endless cycles of growth and decay. He, in his silent way, loved her with a passion that defied his nature. He admired her vivacity, her endless energy, and the beauty she brought to the world.

One day, as she wandered through a meadow bursting with wildflowers, she whispered to the wind, "Why must we be apart? My heart aches for the tranquillity he embodies. I long to feel his touch, just once, to know the peace he offers."

The wind carried her words to him, who stood in the shadows of a weeping willow. His heart, though silent and still, ached with the same longing. He stepped forward, knowing their encounter would bring an end to the natural order. Yet, the pull was irresistible.

They met at the edge of a twilight forest, where the light faded into darkness. Her eyes shimmered with tears of joy and sorrow as she reached out to him. His hand trembled as he extended it towards her.

"Is this the end?" She asked softly, her voice a symphony of hope and fear.

"It is the beginning," He replied, his tone gentle and infinite.

Their fingers touched, and in that instant, a surge of energy pulsed through the universe. She felt an overwhelming peace wash over her, a calm she had never known. He experienced a spark of vitality, a warmth that melted his cold exterior.

For a moment, they were one, a perfect harmony of existence and cessation. But the balance of the world could not bear their union. The sky darkened, and the earth trembled. Her vibrant colors began to fade, and his shadows started to disperse.

Realizing the danger, she pulled away. "We cannot be together," she whispered, tears streaming down her face. "Our love is too powerful, too disruptive."

He nodded, his own form dimming. "But our longing will remain, an eternal testament to what we cannot have."

As they separated, the world returned to its natural order. She continued to bring joy and growth, while he provided rest and relief. Yet, their brief encounter left an indelible mark on the fabric of existence.

Centuries passed, and their yearning endured. She continued to flourish, her heart always aching for her dark, irresistible and enigmatic beloved. She brought new beings into existence, nurturing them with her love and energy. But every sunset, as the world transitioned from day to night, she felt the pull of her unrequited love.

He, too, continued his silent vigil. But each dawn, as darkness gave way to light, he felt the emptiness of his unfulfilled desire.

One fateful day, a mortal woman stood at the brink of her existence. She was old and weary, her life full of memories and experiences. As she lay on her bed, breathing her last, she felt the presence of both her and him by her side. With her final breath, she whispered, "I have lived, and I am ready to die. I see you both, and I understand. Love unfulfilled is the greatest story ever told."

Hearing her words, they realized that their love was not in vain. It was through their longing that mortals found meaning. And so, in the quiet moments between dusk and dawn, they found solace in the knowledge that their love, though unrequited, was the force that bound the universe together.

And in the heart of every living soul, a trace of their love remained, whispering the secrets of the first arrival and the final departure, longing and fulfilment, to those who dared to listen.

XXI
What Remains

In a land beyond the whispering winds and beneath the golden sunsets, there existed a hidden realm known as Enchanted Glade. This magical kingdom was home to the fairies of fairy tales, beings of light and wonder who spun dreams and inspired the hearts of children across the world.

For centuries, the fairies thrived, their wings shimmering with the laughter of children who believed in them. They danced in moonlit meadows, their songs echoing through the stars, and sprinkled stardust on the dreams of little ones. Each fairy had a special role: some painted the skies with rainbows, others guided lost travellers with their glowing orbs, and many whispered stories of courage and love into the ears of sleeping children.

But as time passed, a shadow of sadness crept into Enchanted Glade. The world beyond had changed, and with it, the hearts of children. The magic of fairy tales was fading, replaced by flickering screens and electronic distractions. The fairies watched from their hidden realm, their light growing dimmer with each passing day.

In the heart of the glade, the Fairy Queen, Lumina, called for a gathering. Her silvery hair flowed like a river of stars, and her eyes, once bright with hope, now held a deep sorrow. Fairies from all corners of the kingdom assembled, their wings drooping, and their faces etched with worry.

"My beloved fairies," Lumina began, her voice a soft melody, "the time has come for us to face the truth. The children no longer believe in us. Their dreams no longer seek our magic. We must decide our fate."

A hush fell over the assembly. The fairies, who had once filled the air with laughter and song, now stood silent, their hearts heavy with the weight of lost dreams.

Faye, the youngest of the fairies, stepped forward. Her golden wings fluttered with a glimmer of hope. "Queen Lumina," she said softly, "is there nothing we can do to rekindle the belief in the hearts of children? Perhaps if we show them our magic one last time, they will remember the wonder of fairy tales."

Lumina smiled sadly at Faye's innocence. "Ah, sweet Faye, your heart is pure, but the world has changed. The children's hearts are clouded with new distractions. Our magic cannot reach them as it once did."

A murmur of agreement rippled through the fairies. They knew Lumina spoke the truth. The world had moved on, leaving their magic behind.

With a heavy heart, Lumina raised her wand, its light dimmed by sorrow. "We must depart from this world and find a new home where our light can shine once more. We will leave behind our legacy in the stories and memories of those who still cherish our magic."

Tears sparkled in the eyes of the fairies as they gathered around Lumina. Together, they formed a circle, their wings touching in a final embrace. With a wave of her wand, Lumina released a burst of stardust, enveloping the fairies in a cocoon of light.

As the fairies ascended into the heavens, they sang a bittersweet melody, a farewell to the world they had loved and protected. Their light faded from the glade, leaving behind only a faint shimmer of magic in the air.

In the hearts of those who still believed, a flicker of their magic remained, a reminder that the fairies of Enchanted Glade had once danced under the moon and whispered stories of wonder. And though the fairies had departed, their legacy lived on in the dreams of those who remembered.

For as long as there were hearts open to wonder, the fairies would always have a place to call home.